THE ARRANGEMENT 21

By

H.M. WARD

LAREE BAILEY PRESS
www.HMWard.com

COPYRIGHT

LAREE BAILEY PRESS
First Edition: February 2016
ISBN: 9781630350864

THE ARRANGEMENT 21

Dear Reader,

The Arrangement Series is different. How? The story is organic—and growing swiftly. Originally intended to be four serial novels, fans of the series demanded more Sean & Avery, spurring an entirely new concept: a fan-driven series. When fans ask for more, I write more.

I am astonished and humbled by the response this series has received. As the series grows, I am constantly fascinated by the requests and insights from readers. This series has sold over 10 MILLION copies! The average length of each book is 125 pages in paperback and can be read in a few hours or less.

This series intertwines with my other work, but is designed to be read independently, as a quick read between other titles. You can join in the discussion via my Facebook page: www.facebook.com/AuthorHMWard.

For a complete listing of Ferro books, look here: www.hmward.com & click BOOKS.

Thank you and happy reading!

~Holly

Chapter 1

A soft smile brightens my face, and I can't hide how much I want to say yes. At the same time, a dark thought takes root in my mind, planting seeds of doubt. I can't fathom why I feel that way. It's not Sean. At least, I don't think it is.

I repress my initial grin and search the crevices of my brain for reasons not to get married tonight. One big fat thought springs up like a Pop Tart from the toaster. Holding the ceremony here—in this lunatic's house—seems incredibly wrong.

Sean lifts his hand and runs his fingertips along my cheek. His eyes linger on my face as his hand strokes my skin. "You speak volumes without saying a word." He sounds disappointed, but he doesn't press me.

"Sean—" I want to explain. My joy mingles with shame, and finding words to express my feelings is difficult. I verbally stumble around, jaw flopping like a docked fish, trying to make it clear I'm not rejecting him.

It's not him.

Sean's tender touch is possessive and gentle. It's an enigma similar to the man himself, naked on the giant bed. He's a mountain of muscle and strength, yet he's soft and patient with me now.

"It's just a thought. You don't have to explain Avery." He's quick to speak, pitching his voice low as if my floundering doesn't hurt. But his eyes tell a different story, pinning me in place with their intensity.

The corner of my mouth pulls up, and I drift closer to his face, resting my forehead against his. I wrap my arms around him and clasp my hands behind his thick neck, half naked, my lower parts tangled in the bed linens. "Sean, I'm saying yes. I want to be your wife—I just don't want our wedding here. I don't want Henry standing there while I say my vows. That man tried to..." I inhale a jagged breath, trying not to relive those moments.

My gaze slides to the bed. I focus on the texture of the raw silk comforter, the way it weaves in and out, the way the fibers vary in appearance. Some are thicker in spots, making the weave stand out, smooth and rough combining to form something exquisite.

Sean's fingers are on my chin, lifting my gaze to meet his. His lips are full and soft from sex. The stubble on his face is darker than usual, and the worry typically pinching his brows is, for once, absent. He's afraid, of me, of what I'll say, but he forces his walls down. I want to cry from the sheer beauty of it, knowing it's all for me.

"Tell me what you want. I'll make it happen." He waits, sliding the back of his palm down the side of my neck and brushing my hair over my shoulder before dropping his hand to his lap.

I think for a moment. Two thoughts battle inside my head. One insists that I marry him now—we may never have another chance. The other requires this entire clusterfuck behind us before we commit to something that should be a joyful occasion.

Sean tips his head, catching my eye. "I wish you would talk to me. I know you're thinking something."

"I want both," I tell him. "I want to marry you in a ceremony far away from here, some place we both love. I want to spend our honeymoon basking in your undivided attention." I wring my hands nervously as I speak. "We don't get that, do we?"

"What do you mean?"

"Some people have simple lives, but that's never been true for you, has it? I don't want unrealistic expectations." Besides, I ruined my life plenty, too. Eventually, the ramifications of that will shake out. The only reason they haven't caught up to me yet is because I'm running on adrenaline, boxing and locking my emotions until I can take the time to deal with everything.

He watches me, his blue gaze never leaving my face and nods. "Ask me what you want to know. I hear you dancing around it, but you're too afraid. Ask me, Avery. I'll tell you."

This exposed version of Sean unnerves me. It encourages me to say what I'm thinking, and that's not always a good idea. I don't know what my problem is—it's not Henry—it's not his house. Why am I saying I want a white dress and a happy day? Traditions never mattered to me before, why do I suddenly want them now?

My mouth opens, but I can't find the right words. I look up at him through my lashes, worried. "I—it's not you, or anything you did, I swear it's not. I just have this hunch our lives will always be like this, complicated beyond measure because you're a Ferro." I swallow hard, avoiding his eyes. "I'm a coward, a calloused jerk for thinking it, but it's there. It's like we're cursed." I trip on the "we" part, and it's clear I have a different thought floating around in my mind.

Sean doesn't miss it. Just as the concept materializes in my head, he says it. "You think I'm damned. You think I'll pull you down with me." There's no question in his voice. He pushes off the bed, stands and runs his hands through his hair, leaving me gaping at his naked back. Strong muscles flex, exhibiting his emotions in physical form.

I named the one thing that scares him.

I jump from the bed and duck in front of him, grabbing his hands. His interpretation of my thoughts is slightly off. I feel the walls rising around him. If that happens, I won't get back in. I press my thumbs to his palms and catch his gaze. "That's not what I'm thinking."

"Don't lie to me."

"I'm not. You're wrong, Sean. I love you so much. I'm worried we both have too much baggage. I don't want the things that have happened—or the events yet to be—to crush you. Add in your problems, and the fact that you're a Ferro, paying for the sins of your parents until you die, and it feels hopeless." He tries to pull back, and step away from me, but I don't let him. My hands slip up his arms, sliding along the lean, firm muscles to rest near his elbows. My breasts brush against his lower chest. The height difference between us overwhelms, so I rise on my toes until we're nearly eye to eye.

"I want us to be happy, and I know what that means for you." I take his face in my palms. His walls are somewhere in the middle, not all the way up, but not dropped the way they'd been. "I don't know how to get over this part of my life."

"How do you mean?"

My lips slowly form the words and it's like leisurely pulling off a band-aid. It stings. "How do I reconcile who I am with who I was, with who I wanted to be? I can't forgive myself for my actions. I'm not a good person, not anymore, and I have no excuse. You had horrible things thrust upon you, Sean. None of it was your fault. But this..." I drop back down, my heels sinking into the thick carpet.

"Avery—"

He tries to cut me off, but I keep going. I opened Pandora's box and released all my evil spirits into the world. "Vic, Henry, and Black—I did that. That was all me!"

"You didn't have a choice—"

I laugh bitterly. "I don't deserve you. I don't deserve a happy life." My eyes swipe to the side, and my stomach sinks. "I'm a horrible person. I blamed you for my problems because I couldn't live with myself otherwise—not with my sins. I whored, lied, cheated, stole, killed, and whatever will happen tomorrow."

The unshed tears in my eyes blur the room, making it appear warped. Sean stares at me, frozen in place. I can't read his thoughts, and I'm too afraid to look at his face.

I suck in a shaky breath and spit out the rest. "My own parents would find me deplorable. I'm not the girl I was before this began. I don't deserve a white dress or a sweet little house. I almost screwed that psycho downstairs for money. I didn't mind at the time. What kind of wife would that make me?"

I've been talking so rapidly it almost sounds like a rant. My hands started out flying around, punctuating each thought with a staccato movement. By my final words, my arms wrap defensively around my middle, my hands tucked tightly into the crooks of my elbows, pinned in place.

Head bowed, I realize my problem is me.

I can't accept who I've become.

I don't know how.

I'm not sure if I can.

A moment later, Sean's arms slip around me, holding me comfortingly. I press my face against his chest, inhaling deeply, wondering if he can love me like this. "I'm no longer the girl you met on Deer Park Avenue, chasing her jacked POS car. She's gone."

"Avery—"

"She's not coming back."

"Avery, listen to me." I pull back, face covered in tears and look up at him. His eyes fill with compassion and understanding. "She never left. That's one thing you taught me, and I fought you over it every time you brought it up. The man I was is still inside me, broken and bleeding out, but not gone. Who I am changed, but that part of me—the good part—it's still there. It doesn't die, especially if we don't want it to."

I'm sobbing now, shaking in his arms. "I'm not like you! I did this to myself. I chose it, Sean. You didn't."

"You didn't choose this. You didn't want to be the biological child of a murderer. You didn't ask the adoring parents, who kept you safe for nearly two decades, to orphan you when you needed them most. You didn't set out to make bad choices. You did what was necessary to survive."

I mouth no, begging him to stop. I did this.

But he won't relent. The words keep coming, and it hurts so much to hear the way he talks, like he still has faith in me, like I'm not lost. "Avery, no one faults you for that, least of all me. You showed me compassion when the world only offered scorn. You saw the man I am, and saved me from losing myself, from becoming the monster people think I am—it was all you. That's how I know the girl running down Dear Park Avenue is still alive—she refused to let me go." He kisses the top of my head and holds me close.

I can't stop shaking. The floodgates holding everything back are about to break. There's more misery coming, a tsunami of pain and regret waiting to destroy me. Spoken aloud, my thoughts terrify me. I never let them out, never examining or evaluating my actions, because I know in my heart, I had a choice but made the wrong decisions. I press the gates of my mind closed, holding them there, but they leak. There's no way to seal all the thoughts away until another day.

"How do you live with it?" I ask him. "How do you accept good things as they come your way, especially when you know you don't deserve them?"

"Ah, there's the problem." Sean speaks with a soothing voice as he pulls away from me. He clasps his massive man-hands on my shoulders and looks at my tearstained face. "You don't know who you are anymore. That's all right. It happens from time to time. It happened to me."

"How did you reconcile it? How'd you get back to wanting the baby and the house?"

"You." He smiles with certainty. "It was all you, Avery. You reflected a version of me that was long gone. I couldn't remember how to be that guy, but then you saw all of me—shadows included—and didn't run. You taught me to fight for myself, to consider myself worth saving. You reminded me that

I matter, that I'm loved. I believed you. It's hard not to. You can be very convincing."

I sniffle. "So, you don't want to marry me out of guilt?"

He tosses his head back and laughs. His dark hair falls into his eyes when he looks at me again. He's smiling so voluminously I'm blinded by the wattage. "Avery, I want you to be my wife so I'll be with you at times like this, reminding you who you are and loving you without judgment or regret. I want to revel in your smile when you laugh, to delight in indulging your desires. If I can return even the smallest portion of the happiness you give me, I'll die a happy man."

I can't help it. I grin through the tears. I brush the moisture off my face and feel my heart thumping in my chest. "I'm still alive."

"You are. You wouldn't be without making the choices you did. When most people confront their limits, they break. You didn't. Be proud you held on without falling apart. It's a rare gift."

I'm quiet for a moment, thinking things over. The hole in my heart, that unbearable weight, dissipates as we talk.

I realize it's time for another choice.

Reject his thoughts and self-destruct.

Or believe him and forgive myself.

Chapter 2

My eyes cut to the side and then up to his face. I take a step toward him. "Weirdest ever conversation while naked, right?"

"Well, we once had a discussion about a box that ranked highly on the scale, but this one tops it," he says as he smirks.

"We should get married at The Container Store," I blurt, jokingly.

Sean chokes on his laugh and pulls me into his arms. "That's why I love you. You transform my fucked-up mess into something wholesome. You're my light in the dark shit-storm of life. I adore you." He kisses my temple and rests his head on mine. "I always will."

I feel his content smile, warm against my cheek. Sean figured out how to survive in the present, preventing his past from choking him to death.

Meanwhile, my transgressions rip their way from silent tombs, intent on drowning me. My sins are too great, too awful. I can't outrun the way they're constantly looming, ready to destroy me. At least, that's how I felt at the beginning of this conversation.

I refused to talk about what I did, how I got here, but it still lurks in the dark corners of my brain, poisoning my thoughts.

I savor the warmth of Sean's body, the strength of his arms. In his embrace, I'm at peace. The man who returned me, the man who only appeared for brief glimpses before vanishing now remains in plain sight. Somehow he pacified his past to allow for a future.

I want to be a part of it.

I wrap my arms around him and press my cheek against his chest. Hugging him close, I say, "Yes, I want to marry you, but not tonight. Not here."

He holds his palm to my cheek and assures me. "It's all right, Avery."

"I love you, Sean."

"I love you, too." He clears his throat and sounds more chipper. Sean happy? After being rejected? It's totally weird. "The moonlight is stunning this evening. How about a walk?"

Chapter 3

I wear the ivory chemise meant to line my dress for tomorrow's end game. We're in the garden, walking quietly in the shadows. It's still the middle of the night.

Sean holds my hand, wearing a pair of black tux pants and a matching white shirt. I wonder if they're his or Henry's. They seem to fit him, which releases a whole second set of questions. Sean pulls a lily from the garden and hands it to me. "For you."

The sweet scent fills my head as I admire the pale pink petals. I say I don't like pink, but, privately, I love it. That color makes me smile. It's so girly and cliché that I hate myself for it, but I have worse faults to focus on. "Thank you."

He raises a brow and grins, pulling me to him by my waist. The flower rises between us, its aroma filling our heads. "I know you like pretty things." His lips pull up, those eyes dancing with ideas that make my stomach twist. He leans in close, and whispers in my ear, "Pretty, pale pink things. It's okay. I do, too."

"I can't believe you said that!" I laugh at his innuendo and try to push him away, but he doesn't let me.

"Don't act so shocked. Besides, you like dirty talk, Miss Smith." Sean presses his finger to the tip of my nose.

My spine straightens and I step back, huge grin on my face, jaw hanging open. "I do not."

He cocks his head to the side and gives me a look. "I thought you wanted to learn to live with your dark side. Admit it. Tell me how much you like hearing about my dick doing you any way I want, every time I want you. Like now. I could push you down right here, rip those panties off, and tease you until you beg me to screw you senseless." He touches the side of my face with the tips of his fingers, gazing at me with those dark, sapphire eyes, thinking about ravaging me here and now. His voice is deep, dripping with sex, and he doesn't hide it. He's proud of it, of how much he wants me, of his desires. It makes me breathless.

"Oh, please," I tease, hiding his effect on me. "That's pillow talk for someone like you."

Sean's face shifts and the dark man living inside of him merges with the one who loves me. He steps toward me, and I step back. "Do I need to take you to the shed, Miss Smith?"

I shrug as if he doesn't faze me even though my heart races wildly and the spot between my legs heats way too fast. "That depends. What will we do in there?"

Sean's trying not to show that predatory smile. The corners of his mouth twitch as he steps toward me. His hand juts out and grabs my waist, pulling me forward, slamming me into his hips. There's no mistaking the hard shaft beneath those slacks now pressing substantially against my stomach. I gasp as we collide.

He dips me back slightly, one hand behind my back and the other at my neck. That hot gaze is erratic, darting from my eyes to my lips. He tips my head back, brushing his lips to my ear and I feel his arousal increase.

The warm air and the caress of his mouth make it hard to hide my reaction. I gasp at the sensation of his lips on my skin, wanting more as he pulls away.

His face hosts a carnal look that once terrified me. Honestly, it's still scary. Sean drags me upright and crushes me against his chest. "First, I'll rip this slip from your body, tearing it down the middle and using it to tie your arms above your head. The rafters are low in the shed. You could stand like that, naked, arms bound above your head, those perfect breasts and hot, wet pussy exposed for me to do as I like."

Flutters fill my stomach, but I manage a bored yawn. "Really? Is that all you've got, Box Boy? No dark fantasies you'd rather explore?" I shift my weight, pulling back slightly, letting my breasts brush his chest. Even with the fabric between us, I can tell what it does to him. Though my words are freeing, my actions commit me.

Sean's chest rises and falls as he tries to control his breathing. His body tenses, as if he knows precisely what he wants to do to me. I see it in his eyes, in the way his lips curve into a seductive smile he only uses on his prey. He wets the dark pink skin with his tongue and, as they part, his eyes devour me. A dark fantasy plays out behind his eyes.

"Tell me." My voice catches in my throat. It's not intentional, it's a reaction to his dominance, to the way he's looking at me. A chill slips down my spine, and I shiver.

Sean pulls me to him, slowly, taking one arm at a time, leading me so I rest them on his narrow hips. He holds one hand against my back, palm open, and leans in placing his lips on my ear.

My pulse pounds in my ears, as this provocative scene plays out. My face is blank, staring at him, challenging him in that way he doesn't like, but secretly loves. An alpha asserts control and forces his authority. It thrills me. I admit I like feeling so vulnerable that all I have is trust. It's rare. I don't trust anyone the way I trust him and I never surrender all of myself except in moments when he makes me.

It's a strange feeling I didn't realize I liked at first. Well, that's not entirely accurate. I was appalled that I enjoyed it. I wanted to be dominated by him, but had no idea why. Now I do—it's trust. I know he can push me too far. I know he can break me. But he won't. He'll make my heart pound with ecstasy, forcing me to my limits, commanding me to come harder and feel higher than I thought possible.

I feel his lips part as he prepares to speak. "No," he whispers.

Ah! Fine, if that's how he wants to play it. I pull away, shrug, and smile coyly. "Just as well, I didn't want it anyway."

He grabs me, pulls my front to his, his fingers sliding up my inner thigh, forcing my legs apart. He doesn't ask, he doesn't wait. His fingers slip inside me, pulsing, stroking, teasing. Sean's eyes bore into me. I'm panting, reacting visibly as my body betrays my lie. "Really? Not into it? You could have fooled me. You're dripping. You're so wet that I could drink you." The way he says those last few words is so sexy. His mouth wraps around them slowly, carefully caressing every syllable. It's the pre-show for what he plans to do to me.

I arch my back and push against his hand, lips parted in an "O." A voice too breathy to belong to me teases, "Don't be silly. I get this way around all the guys."

The response is immediate. Sean pushes into me harder, adding another finger, stretching me. My knee rises as I straddle his hip. "You're mine, and I'm the only one who can affect you like this." He moves his fingers inside me, pressing them to a place that steals my breath and weakens my knees. I lean against him as he pulls his hand away.

I'm so turned on I don't see the guy standing a few feet away, beet red, not sure if he should speak or run away. Sean says nothing. It's as if he knew the guy was standing there. I straighten my slip and feel my face flame up.

Slip. Lawn. Nerd. Sean.

Oh, God!

Sean gestures for the guy to come over. When he gets here, my eyes widen. "Asthma Attack, are you okay? Do you need an inhaler?" I'm not trying to be a bitch. I forgot his name. Hell, I forgot my name!

"I'm fine, Miss." He doesn't sound fine.

Then again, neither do I.

My jaw drops. I lean in and whisper-yell, "You knew he was there, didn't you?"

He hears me and hastily says, "I didn't see a damned thing." His face is so red he could be a crayon.

"Then why are you blushing?" I blink at him like he has two heads. He totally saw.

Justin clears his throat and looks at Sean. "The, uh, boulder holder bra provides a nice view for you, but it's a little awkward for me. Of course, I don't have to look." He adds the last part swiftly, and backs up like Sean might break his face.

My slip is smooth silk adorned with lace sewn along the upper cup and hem, an amazing push-up bra up top. When I look down, I blanch. All that flirting left me hot. I didn't notice the lace line on the cups shifted down, exposing the tops of my nipples. Even in the dark, the tops of my nips are clearly visible. I squeak and turn around, adjusting things back where they go. The truth is, when you wear your breasts up around your neck, the girls look great, but they can pop out. It's not like I can tell unless one falls. I'd notice wonky boobs, one up one down—but a popped tit, not so much. It was still in the bra—well, on it.

I'm pretty sure I can smell my makeup burning into smoke and wafting off my face in a little cloud.

Sean's hand is on my shoulder. "He didn't see anything."

I give Sean an incredulous look. "He just said—" I'm jabbing my finger at the guy, horrified when they both cut me off.

Justin is shaking his head like crazy, avoiding my eyes. "I didn't see anything."

"He didn't see that," Sean says, alluding to the thing he did with his hand that had me so hot. Sean smacks the kid in the back of the head. "Anyway, it's not that bad. He was staring at your rack and noticed you're pretty."

They're both lying to me. I laugh, shrugging my shoulders. "It's weird, right? A prude hooker."

Before Sean can reply, Justin says, "You're not a prude, and you're not a hooker. You're Avery Stanz, the woman with balls the size of Texas, the woman taking out Vic Jr. without a second thought." He gets a bashful expression on his face and adds, "Furthermore, you're so beautiful, it's hard to not notice." He flinches. "Sorry, boss."

Sean looks like he wants to kill Justin, but I take Sean's hand in mine, lift it to my lips and press a kiss to the back of his hand. Addressing Justin, I say, "Thank you."

"No problem." He gazes up at me from under his lashes, gets a goofy grin, and resumes avoiding eye contact with Sean. He swallows hard and manages to straighten. "So, are we doing this?"

"Doing what?" I glance between them, not understanding.

"Yes," he says to Justin. "It'll only be a moment, Avery." Sean's voice isn't tense the way I thought it'd be. His expression instantly softens as his eyes cut to the side, to me. The way the moonlight illuminates his face is surreal. It's like he's been kissed by a star on each cheek. Those eyes that undo me are soft and pure. He watches me from behind dark lashes, caught in a moment of bliss.

Chapter 4

Tall oak trees tower above me casting a lacy pattern on the lawn. I kick off my hooker heels because this grass demands bare feet. Sean follows my lead before walking a few paces away with Justin.

Their heads nearly touch, their shoulders leaning forward, and they speak almost noiselessly. The exchange is brief. When Sean turns back around, Justin leaves quickly in the opposite direction. If there were a dog on his heels, he'd be moving slower.

Sean Ferro is a scary man.

He walks toward me, a swagger in his step, and sex in his eyes. He devours me with his gaze and sends a spark up my spine. When he reaches me, Sean laces his fingers with mine. I lean my head on his shoulder for a moment as we walk further into the property, losing ourselves amongst the gnarled trees. I don't trust myself to speak. My throat is too tight. I'm that happy, that emotional.

Sean squeezes my hand as if he knows what I'm thinking. I glance up at him. The hollows of his cheeks are in shadow, making him look delicious. My mind drifts to his threats from a few moments ago.

"Avery?" Sean turns to peer down at me.

"Hmm?" I feel light in that moment, like I could float away on a happy cloud.

Sean laughs softly, and we stop walking. He takes my other hand and tries to hide his smile. He drops to one knee and holds up a ring. "I want to ask you properly. I want you to know how much I love you, how much I will always love you. I want to spend every day with you, and love you every night. I want you by my side, but more than anything, I want to be by yours. You mean everything to me. You're my best friend and lover, mending my fractured soul in a way no one else could. You're my soul mate, my everything. Avery Stanz, will you be my wife?"

I don't mean to, but a deep laugh escapes from somewhere inside my chest. It jumps out of my mouth, and I grin. "That never gets old."

He beams up at me, waiting.

From experience, I know waiting is a bad thing and rush to tell him. "Yes! I would love to be your wife." I feel something swelling inside my chest that's been absent for such a long time. I have trouble identifying it at first. It's not joy or happiness. It's more like a lingering sense of wellbeing, like this will somehow work out.

It's hope.

Sean stands, and when his mouth comes down on mine, I lose myself in him. Our lips burn on contact, igniting everything good within me. I wrap my arms around his neck basking in the moment.

When he pulls away, he's smiling so fiercely I think he might bust. Sean laughs, holding me against his chest and swinging me around. I pull my feet up and squee as I spin in a circle with him on the grass.

When Sean puts me down, he tangles his hands in my hair and holds my face between his palms. "I love you, Spray Start Car Girl. Forever."

Then, without a word, he sweeps me off my feet and lifts me in his arms. I drop the lily on the ground and cling to him. "Where are we going?"

"Where else?"

I grin broadly and try not to giggle. I jut my arm into the air, poking the night sky and proclaim, "To the shed!"

Chapter 5

Sprawling takes on a new meaning. I remember the field at Belmont Lake from when I was a kid. I thought it was big. Henry's lawn makes the entire park resemble a patch of sod. The mansion sits on acreage that spills around the house and deep into the woods. I can't see the fence line, but I'm confident there is one. Henry likes his privacy—probably because he's batshit crazy. It wouldn't surprise me to find naked women trapped beneath the floorboards of his house. He's a little unhinged, and I still want to beat the snot out of him every time he crosses my mind, so I push the thought away.

The grass is cut in a diamond pattern that my Dad would have envied. He was always trying to get the greenest lawn on the block. One summer he fertilized the yard with his own mix of super grow. He had the best-looking yard on the block—and had to mow it three times a week or the grass would have jumped up and eaten the house. I smile remembering it, missing him.

I glance to the right, thinking I saw a light, but it must have been the moonlight reflecting off something—a camera lens maybe? The estate is so big it's not hard to remain concealed while we move around.

"Sean, why aren't you worried about Henry? Don't you think he'll do something twisted, like try and join us in the shed—something I am NOT okay with." I cling to his neck and feel a nervous jitter work it's way up my arms.

Thinking about having sex with dark Sean is like thinking about playing Frogger on the Long Island Expressway at rush hour. It's exhilarating, and I'm sure to get more than I bargained for, like one of those gator-logs that swallow you whole.

I'm biting my bottom lip without realizing it. Gators are freaky creatures. They pretend they can't move fast until they're ready to devour something. If Sean were an animal, he'd be part gator. The log is icing.

Sean's eyes are boring a hole into my head. I feel awkward and wiggle to get down. He holds me tighter. "I'm not putting you down yet, so be still."

"I could get down if I wanted."

"I'm sure." Sarcasm laces his voice.

I twist in his arms and push away. I should land on my feet, but just as I slip from his grip, he bends at the knees, catches me and tosses me over his shoulder.

"Hey!" I kick my feet and push off his strong back, as I try to yell in his face, but I only get the back of his head. He ignores me, pretending like I weigh nothing. "Put me down!"

Instead of being a gentleman about it, his hand comes up and slaps my ass. I wiggle on his shoulder and try to get down. Sean swats me again. "Stop twerking on my shoulder, or I'll do you on the lawn in the big wide open."

I freeze. "I'm not a prude."

He actually laughs. "Are you still on that?"

"NO!" Yes. I am. Why does he think I wouldn't like some PDA? "I think you're a prude."

He laughs, and it shakes his entire body, jostling me on his shoulders. "Me?" Sean stops walking and nearly releases me. "You're playing me." He sounds shocked. He holds me tighter and picks up his pace.

I bounce, hair flopping in my face, strands going in my mouth with my ass sticking out from under my chemise. "Dude, you almost got played." I giggle. "That was fun. Let's do it again."

His hand comes down on my cheeks, harder this time. I kick and try to shift, but his grip is like iron. The air tickles my skin all around the stinging spot. I have the worst wedgie ever. I might as well go commando.

Sean replies, "Let's not."

"Quit hitting me. I don't like it."

"Yes, you do."

I cross my arms and pout. When I realize he can't tell, I flop there, arms dangling down his back like two pieces of spaghetti. I'm staring at his backside as we bob along. Each step makes him flex his tush, curving it into a super-yummy curve. I reach for his waist and tug on his shirt.

"Undressing me, Miss Smith?" He smiles, looking over his shoulder at me. I've got my neck craned around so I can see the jaunty smirk on his face.

I drop his shirt and feign boredom. "Only in your dreams, Mr. Jones."

I flash a show-stopping grin at him. He laughs. "You're in a mood."

"Likewise, captain." My lips curve into a playful smile. "Where the hell is this shed? You've been walking forever. I would have dropped you by now and fallen down dead."

Sean's face scrunches up as if I insulted his manhood. "You can't lift me."

"I did lift you." I jerk my head in an I-told-you-so move and make a face. "How can you not remember?"

"Right. That." He sounds annoyed. "I believe I'd been shot and was concentrating on other things at the moment. Some minor details are fuzzy."

I reach down and slap my hand against his back. I was aiming for his ass, but it's too far away. "Fuzzy! Do you know how much you scared me? Stop getting shot! Also, you're not a dainty guy!"

"Thank God."

"It was like hauling a monster truck through water."

"Water would make it lighter." His voice is light, teasing. "And you should abstain from hitting me unless you want me to retaliate at an unpredictable time."

I shrug. "That could be fun." I grab his shirt in my hand, crumple the fabric as I gather it on one swoop, and smack his skin with the open palm of my other hand. There's a loud slapping sound, and he freezes.

Grinning in a wolfish, still-got-wool-stuck-between-his-teeth manner, Sean replies, "It will be—for me. Keep your hands to yourself, Miss Smith. I can guarantee you won't like the payback."

My stomach twists as a shiver rips through me, making my skin prickle. He notices. "It's not for you."

"Of course not."

I manage to crane my neck long enough to leer at a little house standing on the back corner of the property. "That's the shed?" I squeak. "Can I live there?"

Sean shakes his head and mutters, "Peasants."

"That's not a shed. It's a house! There's an upstairs! Sheds don't have two floors." I glance at it again before I flop down his back.

"This one does, and the upstairs is unfinished with bare rafters rather close to the floor. It makes it so much nicer than standing on a bucket the whole time with your hands tied above your head."

A bucket? I can't tell if he's joking.

A few more steps and we're at the door. Sean swings me down into his arms and cradles me against his chest. His eyes meet mine and hold. There's so much adoration there, such tenderness that it shocks me. I know he loves me, but he never shows it—not like that.

"I love you, my Greek goddess."

My breath catches, and I lose myself in his eyes, unable to rip mine away. I whisper his name and pull his lips to mine. The kiss is tender, soft. He pulls away and watches me as we cross the threshold.

He places me down and follows through on his promise.

I shouldn't be surprised, but the rapid transition from sweetness to darkness shakes me to my core.

Chapter 6

Standing barefoot on the wooden floor, he reaches for my silk slip, grabbing the hem and ripping it in two. It tears like a piece of paper, and I'm in front of the open door in nothing but white panties. An underwire goes flying, and I hear it clatter against the floor, out of sight. I flinch and move to cover myself.

"Don't budge, Miss Smith."

The muscles in my chest freeze as I force my arms back to my sides. I glance at the open door and back to Sean. My fingers graze my bare thighs as I try not to fidget.

Sean drops to his knees in front of me and hooks his thumbs into the sides of my undies. He pulls them over the swell of my hips and past my thighs.

They slip down over my legs and fall to the floor. He presses a kiss to my stomach, as low as possible. I'm not ready for it and tense, sucking in loudly in response.

Sean stands, backs away, steps to the other side of the doorway. His eyes wander over my body, lingering in places as if he's deciding something. I wonder what he's thinking, what he wants to do. His eyes are so dark. The part of his lips combined with the downward tilt of his head give him a dangerous quality. "Turn around."

I could say no. I could tease him and provoke the man standing there, but the expression on his face, the way he hangs his head and flexes his hands slightly as if trying not to—he won't hold back. Not listening will have repercussions. He will have complete control over me.

Glancing around the room, I turn and face away from him. I wrap my arms around my middle and glance over my shoulder, wondering if I'm ready for this. The past few days have been so difficult. It feels like I barely caught my breath, and, if faced with Sean's darker side, I'm not certain I can handle him.

Chapter 7

This building is not a shed. The walls are not metal. There are no rakes, no brooms, and not a lawnmower in sight. The exterior is tumbled brick and stone with little black shutters next to the windows. The interior floors boast scraped hardwood across the entire 3,000 square foot lower level. The wood is stained dark to match the coffered ceiling, which matches the ceilings in the mansion.

If I had to guess, the dark wood up there is mahogany. Who puts exotic wood in a shed? Who would think this was a shed? It's like a big-ass shanty from the Alps. The walls are Venetian plaster with a light wash, and a monster chandelier hangs in the center of the room—instead of the bare bulb most ax murderers use.

Henry Thomas possesses an obscene amount of money. It wouldn't surprise me if his lawn was sliced from emeralds and his trees were covered in black diamond bark.

I'm glancing around, but I say nothing to Sean. There's no furniture in here, no supplies, no seeds, no nothing. It could be a cottage for Henry's mother. Maybe she's under the floorboards in a box!

I cringe inwardly hoping there are no boxes in my immediate future. I talk a good game about the box, but it still freaks me out. It's not like I learned to love small spaces during my time with Sean.

The door is still open. I don't like that mainly because I'm sure Henry can see me. There's no way he doesn't have security cameras. Additionally, a little drone circles the property every few minutes, little green and yellow lights flashing as the thing flies by, buzzing as it goes.

The first time it passes the shed, it ignores me. My gut instinct is that drones are creepy little buggers. But if Constance had used them at the Ferro mansion, would she still be alive? Maybe Sean should invest in drones. If Pizza Dudes can use them to bring you a pie, how bad could they be? Vessels that deliver pizza aren't inherently evil, right?

I could use a pizza. Or cheese. Something. I'm starving.

Sean walks up behind me and puts a blindfold over my eyes, before going upstairs to prepare something horrifying, I'm sure. Waiting, blind makes my pulse pound harder. I'm kneeling, naked on the floor where he left me, hands in my lap and wringing my hands.

The drone whizzes by again, but, this time, I hear the high-pitched sound of the motor buzzing linger. It gets louder like it's going to fly into the room. There's a breeze on my face like I'm about to get hacked with the propellers, and I wince, but before it slashes up my face, it's gone. Creepy mofo. I should wave and punch it if it comes by again. I still need to enroll in ninja classes. I envision myself doing cool things and being a badass, but my execution is a little dodgy.

Back to evil things confusing me—the relationship between Henry and Sean is weird. It's strained, like one of them might snap at any moment and kill the other. I can see it in their stance, how they both assume the posture of a teenage boy with rounded shoulders and utter indifference.

Add floppy hair and a skateboard and he resembles my high school crush. That guy didn't know I was alive. I wonder if he's currently kneeling naked in an empty shed.

Warehouse. It's too big to be a shed. It could be the home of the third little pig.

My knees are starting to ache when I hear the wooden stairs creak behind me. I picture Sean in my mind, descending the staircase, excited and a little worried that he'll break me. As far as I'm concerned, I lived through so much crap the past few weeks that I can survive anything. Physically, I've got it.

Emotionally, maybe not.

I mean, think about it for a second. How am I supposed to reconcile who I wanted to be, with what I've become? How do people stare in the mirror after killing someone? What if that man had a family? They still don't know where he is, that I ended his life. The guy forced my hand. It was him or me, but that doesn't change the way I feel. It'd be the same if I walked into Waldbaum's, picked a random guy and shot him.

I don't kill people.

I'm not a hooker.

I want love, and I found it by selling myself to the man on the staircase. When we have kids, what am I supposed to tell them? Daddy bought Mommy, took her on a date, and purchased the right to take her virginity!

My mind wanders. He played the piano then. We played together. If you remove the whoring part from the story, it sounds sweet. Sean needed me, and I needed him. How we met isn't important.

My blindfold is removed. My senses are suddenly on high alert, and I feel like someone is watching me. I can't see anyone outside, but I can't hear Sean inside either. I glance over my shoulder and find him sitting on the lower step, leaning forward, chin resting on his folded hands. The tux shirt is gone, and the way he sits accentuates his hard, beautiful body. The way the muscles in his arms, swell and curve, wrapping around strength that's buried deep within. It's hard to look away.

"Avery, come here." His voice is softer than usual, as if he's not sure of himself. That's a rare thing for Sean. I rise and pad over to him. When I stop in front of him, he straightens and peers up at me. "I've wanted to do this for a long time, but I don't know if you can handle it. How do you want me to proceed?"

Awkward naked conversation. Whatever he planned, I can tell he wants it immensely. At the same time, the forewarning is freaky. "I need more information than that. What do you want to do?"

This must be something bad, worse than the box and the fake rape. What the hell is it?

His lips part and he relaxes his shoulders and jaw. His eyes avoid me for a moment, and when he meets my gaze again, he offers his hand. "Come and see."

I stay where I am and fold my arms across my chest. Sean stands in front of me, stepping closer, towering over me. His broad shoulders are nearly twice the size of mine. He's in my space, and that cologne fills my head. I breathe in deeply, trying to place the scents. They're warm, strong, and masculine. They whisper of open arms, passionate kisses, and a firm embrace. It's a dance of power and seduction wrapped in the perfect smell.

I step back, which just makes Sean walk forward. He immediately closes the space. I feel his eyes on me, watching me, tracing my curves as he tries not to touch me, not yet.

"Sean, you could show me the things you want to do and they won't seem like a big deal until we're in the moment. It's you. You make the actions beyond comprehension. You make it intense, igniting the room with your presence. I don't think showing me will help. You need to decide how much you want this—if it's worth it to you."

Before his gaze drops, I see the conflict warring within him. Love isn't supposed to be this way, but for him, it is. It always will be. Part of him suffered in darkness so long he can't simply walk away. I don't know if it's love or insanity on my part, but I know he needs this and I want to be there for him. Plus I kind of like it, but I'm not ready to admit that out loud yet.

He lets out a rush of air and runs his hands through his hair and down the back of his head. He stays like that for a moment, arms held tight at the nape of his neck watching me, thinking. He's wondering if I can take whatever he's planning to do.

He clears his throat and drops his hands, shoving them into his pockets. "I was involved in some pretty messed up things in the past, Avery."

I want to say, 'I know,' but I don't know specifics, and I don't want to hear about how he fucked some girl on a cactus while she was screaming and terrified.

I press my lips together and lift my chin. "I know you had to do what you needed to do to stay sane. Is this for sanity or recreation? Who's asking me if I can handle this? Survivor Sean or Fun Times Sean?"

He doesn't speak which is answer enough.

He thought I was dead. He thought my brother killed me and mutilated my body. I thought the same of him. I thought Vic killed Sean, and I had lost him forever. I don't want to be without him. I don't want to make him deal with this alone.

I rest my hand on his elbow after taking a step closer. Looking up into his face, our eyes meet and hold. My stomach flips and falls to the floor shattering like a china bowl when I speak. My brain and my heart battle, but my brain is defeated. It's waving flags like a lunatic running across a battlefield, more likely to get killed than solve anything.

RED FLAGS.

Everywhere.

I see them exploding. The tattered fabric waves from the end of the pole, burning. Fire slowly consumes the cloth until there's nothing left.

It's one of those times my mind operates on instinct, showing me what will happen if I do this—it solves nothing, and his pain will still be there in the morning. I'll only destroy myself in the process.

"Let's go," I say, trying to hide the tremor in my voice. "Take what you need and don't ask me again. My answer is yes."

Chapter 8

The crazy chick inside my brain is dancing naked with the burning flag. She skips around like a cracked-out banshee, enjoying this. I chose it, right? I should like things I select for myself. I love Sean, but OMG.

I'm standing in the upstairs room and glancing around. The floors are polished stone, and the walls are bare, except for some racks hanging from the ceiling. They seem like they should hold rakes and shovels, but they're empty. Where the hell are brooms!

There are no windows up here. No clock. Very little light. No chandelier. The stone beneath my feet is chilled, but it's not what has me frozen in place. It's something else, something resembling a pool, but I'm not that dumb. It's a slim, clear case about five feet tall, with a hinged top that stands open. Above it dangles a narrow pipe that almost looks like it belongs on a kitchen sink. My eyes fixate on the holes in the lid of the plastic prison.

My heart is ready to tear out of my chest and run the fuck away. We are so far past nightmare territory. It's a combination of dreams, fears, and reoccurring horrors I try to erase from my mind on a daily basis.

Worry pinches my brow no matter how hard I try to act like this is normal. Because everyone builds a shed with a torture chamber in the attic on their property. I don't realize I'm holding my breath until I suck in a gasp and feel my lungs burn.

"I can't do this." Terror streaks through me, crying out for sane Avery to save me from the naked nut dancing in my mind, chanting that I can do anything!

Sean grabs me by the wrist, preventing me from bolting butt-naked across the yard. At this point, Henry Thomas seems sane. Then again, this is his house.

Sean's voice is firm. "We talk. We never run away. Sit." He points to the floor, and the command sounds a little too dog and master for me.

"Do you—? That's what nightmares are made of, Sean!" I stutter, pointing—not sitting—and trying to make my mouth say real words, because holy fuckbunnies! No! I shake my head vigorously and step away from him.

"Avery, you don't even know what I want to do." He smiles like this is funny.

I slap his chest and yell at him. My head aches as I scream with my hands balled into fists at my sides. "This is not all right! I can't even fathom how this is here, why there's an Avery-sized fish tank in Henry's shed." I blink furiously and bellow, "Wherearethebrooms!" It comes out in a crazy rush so that it sounds like one word. My arms are tense, and I fling them out in front of me, palms up, making a very logical point with a very irrational man.

His response is a soft smile and light laughter. He grins so adoringly at me that a dimple appears on his cheek beneath all that scruff, along with a lopsided smile that's more coy than menacing. He tries to take my hands, but I scream something incoherently, and he backs away. "You want a broom? Why?"

"You think I'm asking weird questions? Are you fucking serious? Why is that tank the same size as me? Why are there plastic thingies that appear very similar to manacles right where my hands would be? Why Sean?" I get up in his face and poke his chest. I feel crazy, like I should run away.

"Stop thinking. This is about feeling."

"I FEEL NOT ALL RIGHT!"

Still smiling, he steps toward me with a scrap of silk in his hand. "Then stop looking." He moves behind me, lifting the piece of my former slip and placing it over my eyes.

As he's tightening it, getting ready to tie a knot, my hand darts up and jerks it away. Whirling, around, I plead, "You won't hurt me. Promise me that, say it." The words are all air, and I'm beyond panicked.

Sean reaches for my face, cupping my cheeks. "Do you trust me?"

I watch him for a few moments without speaking. I do, but this is too much. I finally feel myself nodding. Sean moves behind me again and ties the blindfold in place.

Chapter 9

I expect my wrists and ankles to follow, but he remains at my back and pulls me to him.

His body is hot, and his skin is slightly damp with sweat. It makes me wonder what he was doing before I came up. His voice is in my ear, but his hands travel from my outer thigh over the swell of my hips and to my waist. "Breathe for me. Slowly, deeply." I feel him inhale, his chest pressing to my back as he does it. I'm close to shaking, but I manage to take the next breath with him. We breathe together and by the third breath, I'm no longer shaking.

His hands begin to roam, sliding over my skin, tenderly sweeping his palm over my breasts and then down to my waist again. His neck is next to mine, his lips right by my ear. His breath is warm and perfect. I feel his whiskers against my skin when he moves, as he breathes.

Worry pinches my brow as I start to think about the tank again, and Sean can tell. His voice is in my ear, "Stop thinking."

"I'm not."

"You are." He nips my earlobe, pressing the soft flesh between his teeth and grazing the skin. I gasp, not expecting the accompanying swirling sensation in my lower body. His lips travel down my throat to the hollow of my neck where he licks my skin with gentle strokes of his tongue.

I melt. My knees no longer want to hold me, and the worried girl runs off with the flag chick, leaving my thoughts on nothing but the way I feel at that moment. His hot lips on my neck do something to me. It's that spot, nearly to the back, that turns my knees to jelly and makes my head feel woozy. I could get lost in that kiss, forget who I am and where we are.

There's a veil that can't be seen fighting to cover my mind from within. The longer his lips stay on that spot, the more I moan and reach back for him. I touch his hair, tangling it in my fingers, pulling. My back arches away from him, but that only makes Sean hold on tighter. His lips devour me, his tongue working that place until I can't stand.

I don't know how he moved me, but I'm pressing face first into a wall. The cold plaster makes me suck in audibly, but that sensation is fleeting. Sean's hands travel up and down my body as he battles me for control of my mind. That spot is so sensitive, so vulnerable. I feel a haze try to descend on my subconscious, but I won't allow it. It nearly swallows me whole when his hands cup my breasts. It comes close to overtaking me when his hand slips between my thighs, pressing me harder to the wall, stealing my breath away.

I shiver beneath him, wishing I could let go the way he wants. I did it before, but it's rare. As much as he likes control, so do I. Letting that irrational nude dancing girl overtake me sounds like an insanely stupid idea, but his lips and the repetitive smooth stroking of his hands convince me.

A sound comes from the back of my throat as my head tips back against his shoulder. I press my hips down, craving more pressure. He has me so turned on, so hot. I stand there blindly, facing the wall with my hands rooted to the plaster like a cop is patting me down in a very naughty way.

His lips pass over that sensitive spot, and my knees give out. Sean's leg presses between my legs and holds me up, pressing me to the wall. I can't stop thinking about taking him in my mouth, kneeling in front of him, and doing anything he wants.

The tank.

I can't stop thinking about it. I don't want to go in there. I can't let him do that to me. My eyes flick open, and I'm staring at cream-colored silk. I reach to pull the blindfold off, but Sean grabs both my wrists and pins me to the wall.

I feel him close to me, his warm breath in my ear, "That stays on, Miss Smith, and if you want your hands free, I suggest you listen. Keep your palms on the wall when I release you."

I do as he says and then feel a cold rush of air on my back. He's stepped away. His voice comes from somewhere behind me. "Spread your legs shoulder width apart. Keep your hands where they are, and don't move."

My heart is racing and my body flushes with heat. Something dark and delicious is swirling inside me. It toys with the idea of letting the veil drop, of letting Sean take me higher and letting go. To just feel good for a while would b—

The thought is cut off when I notice his breath on my inner thigh. A moment later his face is pressing against my lower lips and his tongue sweeps between them, licking me with one wet sweep. I shudder and call out to him. I always want to touch him when he does that. My hands don't want to stay on the wall.

There's a sharp sting on my left butt cheek. He flicked me with something. It felt like hard fabric—a piece of leather? "Hands on the wall, high above your head. Lean forward, baby."

I do as he says, and realize as I lean forward, my back curves and forces my ass out. He's there again, between my legs, kissing me in places that make it difficult to stand. His rhythmic licks steal my breath, and when he presses his tongue deep within me, I wish I had something to grip. I clutch the wall and try so hard not to move, but I want to grind against his face. I want to feel my body become one with his, tensing around him over and over again.

I gasp his name and his tongue changes rhythm, does something else that makes my eyes close and my breath hitch. He likes to watch, to see what he does to me.

I finally understand his draw to the tank.

Sean brings me close to the edge but doesn't push me over. He stands at my back again, trailing kisses across the rises and falls of my body. He finds another spot that makes me breathless. My knees tremble, and his leg juts out, catching me. I grind against his knee as he kisses my back. His hands move up toward my breasts, and he holds them, stroking my taut nipples gradually. He teases them into erotic twin peaks, pleasuring me in ways I have no words to describe

My head tips to the side as the rest of my thoughts fade away. He lifts his head and trails kisses back to that mind-numbing slut button on my neck. I don't care this time. I don't fight him for control. His hands roam over my body as his lips press against that pulse point. The lusty fog clouds my mind again, rolling in low and filling the space, obscuring everything else.

I let it overtake me. I stop fighting against the feelings Sean's trying to show me. I go limp in his arms as my last bit of logic leaves my body. I can't see, I only feel. The V at the top of my legs is hot, pulsing, begging for things he hasn't offered. My lips swell as I consider turning and falling to my knees, and taking him in my mouth, sucking him as his hard length passes over my lips again and again. I want to taste him, to feel that hot, sweet part of him fill my mouth and drip down my throat.

Before I can do any of that, he sweeps me up in his arms and walks me across the room. I hang my head back, dangling it from his arm, not caring where we're going as long as he's with me. The terror that box inspired tries to break through, but I'm too far gone to care.

He sets me down, pressing against me until I step back. Cold bracelets close around my wrists. They're thick, and I know where I am, but I can't picture how he put me in that cell. Another strap closes around my throat, and the last is a belt around my waist. Panic begins to seep back through and it's as if Sean senses it. He presses his body to mine, and I can feel how hard he is, how much he wants me. He whispers in my ear, "Trust me, Avery. Let go, and stay there. Control your fear."

Then he's gone. Something cold presses against my breasts, belly, and thighs as I hear a latch click shut. I breathe in sharply, tensing as the sound of water follows. It comes from above, dripping over my face in a thin stream, while also flowing up from below, the warm water around my ankles rising evenly.

The air is stagnant, and I know the box is closed. The only air comes in from the top where I saw the holes earlier. I flex my hands, stretching my fingers as water trickles down my fingertips and splashes into the rising waters below.

It's my nightmare, the one where I drown. The water from above trickles over my mouth streaming from side to side, making it feel like there's not enough air as the box fills from below. The level is still rising, passing my knees and bypassing places pressed painfully against the transparent walls.

He's watching. Sean is sitting there observing me, waiting for me to scream, to beg him to save me. At least, I think he is, unless he's got something worse planned.

My pulse races as I thrash my head from side side, trying to avoid the water rolling down my f in sheets. I gasp and pull at the restraints on wrists. I don't want to remember the one around neck. I don't want to think about how it feels like hand crushing my throat even though it's not.

The water level passes my breasts and the swallows my body up to my shoulders. As it creeps up my neck, I try to go slack. I try to lose myself in the lusty thoughts that filled my mind before, but I can't. The blindfold is soaking wet, and I can see through the fabric. There's a dark outline of a man sitting before me, watching me. He's blurred, but all the same, I know he's there. Just like I can feel how close my face is to the glass, how my warm breath rolls back over me every time I exhale. The water creeps up my neck like a noose, rising, creeping closer to my lips. I need to scream, but I don't.

When the water licks my chin, I lose it. I pull against the neck restraint, but I can't move. He's not going to stop it. The water will keep rising. He's going to hold me underwater. A scream rips from within and pierces the room, echoing off the empty walls. Frantically, I pull trying to free myself, and only manage to make my throat hurt.

As the water rises higher, I tip my head back, but there's no room. It barely moves. The water line is at my lower lip threatening to spill into my lungs and

drown me. Sean moves. He rises and walks toward the crate. The water stops rising, but the bindings suddenly tighten. My chin lowers and the water rises to my nose. I can't move. I can't scream.

My hands flail in vain, unable to escape. Panic widens my eyes as the water suddenly gushes over my head. My hair lifts and I hold my breath. I'm a mess of terror and lust, and my body no longer responds to me. It strains against the bindings, trying to save itself.

I still when I feel him slide against me, his warm body somehow in the tube with me, pressing firmly against my body. His hard length scrapes against my stomach until he lands his feet on the floor of the cube.

My lungs are burning so terribly I'm ready to suck in water when it quickly vanishes. I'm left tethered to cold hard plastic, unable to move anything except my feet.

When the water's gone, I try to cough and scream, but his lips are there, on mine. He shoves his knee between my legs, parting my thighs before taking me by my hips so that I'm straddling him. As his lips work my mouth, he pushes inside of me. He's hot and hard. He doesn't ask or wait. He doesn't do anything except fuck me hard.

I hate not being able to move and I still feel choked. I'm dripping, and so is he as he pushes into me over and over again. I'm furious and fearful, but

what shocks me is the sensation building beneath the rage. I'm a wet doll, tied in place, but every time he pulls out, I want him back. My heels lock behind his back and I make a high-pitched protest.

I touch my hand to the wall, steadying myself as every part of me trembles with lust, wanting more. There's nothing else, only him and me. I push my hips against him, saying things I'd never admit I said, begging him to do things to me I had no idea I wanted.

He spreads his hands on either side of my head and rips off my blindfold with his teeth. "I want to watch you come."

His eyes reflect a tortured animal, one that never touches, never trusts. He's been hurt too many times, too deeply. He chains his prey up to keep her from giving affection. He doesn't want her that way.

Sean stills and begins to grind into me in a circular motion that makes me want more. "Don't stop," I beg, my voice breathless.

He doesn't. I close my eyes and let him finish me off, gyrating that huge cock deep inside me, pressing it harder and faster, penetrating every part of me until the tension building inside me releases. He stills, hangs his head back and feels me coming. The hard pulsing doesn't stop right away, and before it can slow, he's fucking me again.

I don't have a chance to come off my high. I don't have a chance to collect my shattered pieces. Instead, he takes me higher, pumping into me as his lips find that spot on my neck. The world goes white. Whatever lusty fog crept in before isn't the same as this. I'm lost, completely gone. I don't fight the bindings. I like them. As he pushes into me deeper, pressing his shaft against my delicate nub of flesh as he slides slowly in and out, slowly, exquisitely, I feel like an animal. It's horrifying and freeing.

I beg him to take me in every way possible. I describe what I want him to do to me, and how desperately I want it. While I speak my breasts become tender, aching with need. I tell him to suck me there, to drag his teeth along my skin and nip me. I want more. I need him more than air, more than light. The darkness that was crushing me is gone, and I'm his alone. I want to be used and fucked until I can't stay awake. And then I want more.

Sean comes up for air, breathless, and dripping with water. "I knew you'd like a collar. Tell me what you want, baby."

"I want you, all of you. Now. Come inside of me, fill my mouth. Let me suck you."

He listens and then silences me with his mouth. He doesn't do what I want, which makes me beg more when he steps away. His body is glistening, and I want to touch him, dig my nails into his chest and pull down hard. I want to hear him scream my name and beg for more. He sees it in my eyes and grins at me.

"Cum slut."

The corners of my mouth twitch. "If you ever mention this, I'll deny it."

"I don't care if you admit it or not, as long as you know how much you want it—how much you want me like this." He pulls over a small table that was at the far end of the room and climbs on it. His dick is so close to my face. I open my mouth and try to take it in, but he doesn't let me.

Instead, he remains just out of reach. I pout and watch him as he pulls something out of the drawer—oil. He rubs it on his shaft, taking it in his hand and pumping his hand up and down.

Sean lowers himself slightly and reaches for my breasts. He holds them together as he pushes his hard length between. He slides between my girls repeatedly as his fingers tighten around my nipples, teasing them. Sean dips his head back and makes a guttural sound in the back of his throat. He's so hard, so close.

More things, more requests I thought I'd never say. "Come on me, and then feed it to me. I want to taste you when you're done."

He doesn't say anything, he just does it. Sean forces his dick between my breasts hard and fast, fucking my girls hard. He shudders, and I feel the warm trail of sweetness as he slows his hips, pressing into me one last time, covering me in him.

Breathless, he rises to his knees and holds himself out to me. I can't quite reach. He does it on purpose—he must. He moves his wet cock along my lips, watching me as I struggle against the collar, trying to take him in my mouth. He finally pushes himself between my lips and moans.

I'm engulfed by sensations and emotions so intense I wish my hands were free so I could worship his dick the way I want. It's perfection, smooth and hardening again with every flick of my tongue. He growls, gripping both sides of my head. He presses himself over my lips and down my throat, moaning my name, saying how sexy I am for taking the length of him at once. Every last inch of him is in my mouth, tip to base. I stroke him with my tongue and he rocks into my face, fucking me the way I wanted.

As he grows harder, he gets thicker, longer. His thrusts become more forceful and I want him to do it. I want all of him, nothing held back. He pounds into me three times, then holds his cock in place. He gasps, and his voice is liquid sex. "I can't believe you did this to me."

I feel the pulsing, and he pulls back. I suck hard to keep him there, wanting more. Sean slides the tip of his dick over my lips, pushing it into my mouth, and I suck hard, trying to pull him all the way in before he pulls out again. He makes a sexy sigh of resignation and holds my face, pumping into me, pushing all the way in until I feel him pulsing and coming in my mouth. I suck him savagely, milking every last drop from him, and when he pulls away, I lick my lips.

Sean leans on his side, gasping, covered in sweat. "Oh my God, Avery. I never—" He flops down on his back and covers his face with his arm, still breathing hard. "God, that was amazing."

Chapter 10

Morning comes and goes. Sean is asleep next to me in the blood-colored bedroom once again. We planned to stay up last night, wearing ourselves out until we passed out this morning in order to sleep before tonight. The thing is, I can't sleep. There are no nightmares. I just can't doze off. I lie here, staring at the ceiling, wondering about everything.

Like Henry. He was such a great guy when I met him. I wonder which version of him is real, the dashing English nobleman or Jack the Ripper. Maybe he was high or something the night he went nuts on me? His intolerance of Sean is obvious, regardless of everything else.

Why do I care if he's a good guy or a bad guy? I'm with Sean.

It's not about that. Thoughts start to simmer at the back of my mind. They have no words yet, no pictures to help me discover what I'm thinking. Then there's a bubble of truth—it's about you, Avery. Then another—picking paths. Soon the pot is boiling, and I can't stop it. My mind wraps around the hot pot with nothing to keep it from searing my skin. My heart pounds harder and my breathing shallows. Suddenly it's too hot, and I don't want to think about it anymore. But the thought is still there, plain as a black mark on a white page.

Vic Jr., my brother, had to start somewhere. People aren't born evil.

Constance. Sean's mother, she had to be kind as a girl. People choose paths.

Mom. The woman I knew wouldn't be in bed with a guy like that, never mind everything else. I didn't know her as well as I thought. I faulted her for things I was clueless about.

Sean. The man sleeping next to me was once a wide-eyed little boy with no nefarious thoughts at all.

Mel. Surviving justifies anything.

Isn't that what they all have in common? Isn't that why I feel an anxiety attack ready to bop me in the back of the head like a two by four? Because it's not just them and they didn't do this to me, to my life—I did. I made my choices, and I have to live with the consequences. Trying to outrun them turns people cold, like Constance. Reveling in it leads down my brother's path. He's a bloodthirsty nut. If he had a brother instead of a sister, I doubt incest would be on his mind. Or necrophilia. Maybe it would be. Sex is power, and that guy is power thirsty. He'd do anything and everything to get it. I shudder under the blankets even though the room is warm.

It's past noon. I can tell from the way the light cuts through the center of the drapes, casting a long golden slab of light on the dark carpet.

I watch Sean for a moment and want to ask him where he was the night he came back covered in blood, what he did, but I know better. Leave the past in the past. Bury it and walk away.

There's a problem with that theory of dealing with life. Inner conflicts, thoughts, and actions never shown the light of day have a way of turning into something dark and despicable in the shadows. Demons will kill you faster than anything else. I have a hissing gaggle of them following me around, waiting for me to crack—that thought terrifies me most—because I know who I'll become.

Chapter 11

I have on a pair of sweats I found in the closet. I don't want to ponder on the size of the women's clothing or that tank. It's like Henry stocked his house with Avery-sized things. I shake my head and banish the thought.

Good people can do bad things. I already have, but if things get out of hand tonight, can I do what I need to do? Can I execute the Plan B Mel and I created? Can I deviate to my own sick, twisted plan and end this once and for all?

Vic isn't only aiming for me. He's got sights on Sean, his brothers, Mel, Marty, Henry, and even Gabe. Memories of the gruff old man pass behind my eyes as I wander the empty house. He told me so many times to get away from Black. She's the one who started this. She's the one who moved from selling sex to selling murder. I blame her, but she's a distraction. She needed Vic to pull this off. If we take him down, that'll end it.

If I take Black out, too—I cut off both heads. I'm not new here, I know the heads will just grow back, but it'll take time. In the meantime, everyone in New York with a price on their head can breathe easy, their debts forgiven.

I'm walking along an upper corridor with a cup of coffee in my hands. My hair is pulled back into a messy ponytail, and I'm barefoot. I sip the cup as I stare at the madness on the walls. Henry's infatuation with Henry VIII is concerning. This particular passage shows his timeline, from young boy, to idyllic young king, to insanity. He took what he wanted and left a path of carnage in his wake. He killed his best friends and advisors—and, of course, his wives. I knew he killed them to bypass the divorce issue, as if that justifies murder, but I didn't understand the accusations. As I travel down the hall, I see the list of crimes and cringe. I wonder if the king himself thought up those charges or if the power hungry people around him did it. Either way, this wall shows a good man's descent into Hell.

I wonder what my wall will include.

"Avery?" Marty's voice is soft, as if he didn't mean to startle me. I turn and almost don't recognize him. His head is shaved, and there's a gash on his temple with fresh sutures. He's wearing black cargo pants and a dark gray shirt with something resembling Kevlar woven into the fabric over his chest and torso. "I didn't know you were up."

My eyes go wide, and I rush him, yelling a million things at once. "Where were you? I thought you were dead!" I crash into him and pound my fists on his chest. It feels like he's back from the dead. I didn't even want to think about where he's been.

Marty stands there like I'm some crazy girl he ran into at the mall, as if I shouldn't be upset. "I'm here now."

I make a strangled sound in the back of my throat and slam both palms on his chest. "Where were you? Don't do that to me, again." I deflate and suck in a sharp breath, and step away another pace.

He swallows hard, looking at me as if he wants to say something. He finally shoves his hands in his pockets and talks. "I had a situation with Vic's men after I pulled Sean off the beach. He was pretty banged up, and I couldn't stay with him. Long story short, I made up some bullshit and then ran after you. By the time I got back to the beach, Vic was beyond pissed. That fucker did this with his gun." He points to the stitches above his eye. "I'm surprised he didn't pull the trigger."

"Oh my God." I stare at him, horrified. "Why did he let you go?"

"I convinced him he still needs me. I may have threatened to expose him, too. I expected to die, so I said whatever sounded good. Apparently saying fuck-ass crazy crap appeals to the man. He laughed, slapped me on the back, and sent me to find you."

"Where have you been, then?"

"Hanging back, making sure Vic isn't following me. I didn't come here until I knew I'd lost them for a few days."

There are things I want to ask him, lingering questions that won't fade away. I still have no idea if I should hug him or hit him. He was supposed to kill me. Does the fact that I'm still breathing negate that whole thing? He lied so many times.

So have I.

I shake off my disgust. In many ways, we are the same. Besides, he kept me alive, and that's hard to overlook. I shove the thought aside and lock it away under my mental floorboards with the rest. I'm wholly aware there will be a huge-ass tidal wave of bad crap coming one day, and that's the thing—I know it's not today—so I stuff it away.

"So, I thought you were supposed to be sleeping. Henry filled me in about tonight."

"Yeah, I couldn't sleep." My grip on the mug tightens, and I try to focus on the warmth radiating through the porcelain walls.

He nods, but his eyes don't leave my face. There's something about the way he stands that makes me think he has a lot to say, conversations the size of mountains, words I don't want to hear. He knows things about my parents, about my mother. There's also softness there, something in the corner of his eyes, hanging like a tear that never falls. He still cares about me. After everything that happened, he's not over me.

I'm a train wreck of emotions and regret. How can he still think of me as pure-hearted and perfect? What happened to the Marty who dressed by the decade and made me smile? Was that an act for my benefit? The man is an assassin, and he's too smart to be here now, but he is.

Marty stands there, feet a shoulders width apart, hands clasped behind his back like a soldier. Why didn't I see it before? The overcompensation, the way he slouched all the time, and his dramatic movements. He spoke volumes with his hands, and each expression held a myriad of thoughts. I thought it was because he was gay and wanted people to know. I accepted the act as genuine, assuming I knew the reason.

Everyone wears a mask from the time they wake up to the time they pass out every night. Some are acceptable, others, not so much. People can't be real, because when they are, when they say what's truly lurking in their hearts, they're people like Vic and his dad. People who hide nothing about how they think or feel. That scares most people, myself included.

This might be the last time we speak. Say it, Avery. If you want to know so much, ask him.

Before I can speak, Marty inclines his head toward the wall. There's a painting of Jane Seymore, Henry VIII's third wife. "Not much is known about her, except that she seemed to be able to navigate Henry's dark past without making it explode. Her epithet calls her a phoenix, a bird reborn from its ashes."

I stare at the light brown liquid in the cup. I don't think I like where this conversation is going. I force my gaze up and let it harden. "Don't tell me you have a fascination with the murdering king, too."

"When a person's life slips away from the light, they have to find a way to make peace with it. Everything around us says one thing, but the masses are sheep. People who can think are screwed if they follow the flock. You're not a follower, Avery. I know you."

The last three words hang in the air. He knows I'm thinking about deviating from our plan. He knows how I feel about everything I've done. He suspects I've done worse than I said, but he never pries, never asks.

"I'm not going rogue tonight, so you don't need to worry about that." I begin to walk away, but he reaches out and takes my arm. I stop and gaze up at all six-plus feet of him.

He laughs jadedly. "Tell me. Let another person in on your suicide mission."

"It's not like that, and I did. Mel knows, and she helped me with it. If things don't work out, then I have a Plan B."

"Right, and what about Plan C? Don't pretend with me. I know you struggle with all the shit that's come your way, and I'm shocked you held it together this long. But Vic isn't the guy to test how far you can go. He'll ruin you."

"I don't know what you're talking about. There is no alternate plan beyond that." I go to walk away, but he jerks my arm, spilling coffee on the rug.

Marty gets in my face and leans down, lowering his voice. "I've known you longer than him." He points back in the general direction of Sean's room. "He's missing this. You're going to implode. You're creating a meticulous plan to take out all your adversaries at once. There's always carnage in the area surrounding a blast. You want to make the most of it, which means you're thinking something horrible. For me to say it's horrible, as in a nauseatingly, blood-curdling idea, then it's really bad. You know me, and I know you."

My mouth goes dry. I stand there staring into his face and feel ice dripping into my stomach. I can't think about tonight. It'll make me sick, but somehow Marty managed to lock on something everyone else missed. It's not a death wish, not exactly. It's more pragmatic than that. The only way I can make sure every single person involved dies is to die with them. I can't find another way around it.

I remember to breathe and place my hand on his forearm, making him drop my elbow. "What do you want from me?"

Marty steps back, making an exasperated sound as he drags his hands down his face. "I'm not having this conversation with you again. We've had it twenty times already." He steps toward me, closing the space between us. "I can't let you do this. If that means fucking up their plans, so be it. I'll take you from them, here and now, and never let you go."

The desperation in his voice makes me believe him. I stop pretending it's not true. He thinks too much like me. He knows me too well to deny it. I need him as an ally, not an adversary. I pull him down the hall by his arm to a spot I'm sure no one else can hear or see us. There are no windows, no rooms, and the hallway dead ends under a big painting of King Henry VIII as a young man.

Marty lifts his brows, waiting for me to speak. He's beyond irritated, and I think he might make good on kidnapping me. I have to talk him down, and the only way to do that is to include him in my plans. But he cares about me. That part is going to make him unbalanced. If Sean were going to do what I'm planning, I'd threaten kidnapping, too. A brick to the brain is safer than my plan.

"Marty, I know you think I'm an idiot, but—"

"No, I don't. I think you're on a mission to annihilate anyone who fucked with you, myself included. I could get behind that, accepting whatever is coming to me, but not at this cost. You're not factoring everything into the equation."

"Yes, I am."

"No, you're not. The question isn't what are you capable of? It's what can you live with if you survive? Say by some freak chance you make it out alive—"

"I won't."

"You don't know that. Anything could happen when you put Black and Vic in a room together. For all you know, it could turn into a three-way or the two of them could feed you to the bear."

That makes me pause. I straighten, blinking too many times. "Vic has a bear?"

"It's white with freaky pink eyes. He likes hearing people scream, Avery. That fucker could do anything, and I mean anything. He has no mercy, and his soul is long gone. I think he was born evil. He likes to tell the story of how he killed his mother, and the things he did with her—with her body and her blood—" his face twists with disgust. "He liked her, Avery. Vic hates you."

There's only one way to leave this hallway that doesn't end with a kidnapping. "Then help me, and I swear to God if you tell anyone about this, I'll make you wish you hadn't."

His eyes are wide and warm, like melted chocolates. "You never need to threaten me. I'll give you anything you ask for, do anything you want. Just say you want my help." He watches me with such intensity that my skin prickles and a shiver works its way up my throat.

I've never had someone pledge allegiance to me before, not like this, not when I wasn't in love with him. Marty knows it, and he's still here. Guilt tries to overtake me, but I take a mental shovel to its head before I feel it. My shed has stuff in it.

Swallowing hard, I say, "I want your help, Marty."

Chapter 12

I feel like I made a deal with the devil, and it doesn't sit right with me. I'm missing something, and I can't put my finger on it, but if I don't get the last puzzle piece before tonight, I'm screwed.

I tell Marty my plan and watch his lower eyelid twitch as I explain what I'm willing to do to finish this. He clears his throat and tries not to strangle me. He licks his lips, unclenches his hands, and takes a deep breath. "What makes you think he'll be okay with that?"

"It was okay last time he tried to kill me, so I'm guessing that he's still thinking about it."

Marty's mouth is in a straight line, and his lean arms tuck tightly into the crooks of his arms. I speak so softly, he's forced to lean in close to hear me. I couldn't admit this to Sean. Hell, I can barely admit it to me. Dark ideas hide out in my brain, and they're twisted enough to make Marty uneasy.

That's what I mean, about what I was thinking earlier. I'm Vic's sister, and my father was equally deplorable, albeit a little less crazy than his son. It's a slippery slope, and I'm already on it, sliding down on my backside, ready to hit bottom.

Marty lifts a hand to his jaw. It keeps the fist shape, and he holds it under his jaw, staring into space as he thinks. "It's better than I expected, but there are a few things you can do to tighten it up. I'll make sure Sean stays away, but you're on your own if this goes to Hell. If it doesn't, living with that is going to be—"

"If it goes that far off track, I won't have to live with it."

"Avery—"

"Marty, I made up my mind. It's not a matter of what I can do. You said it yourself. The heart of the matter is what can I live with. This plan is so far outside of who I am and who I want to be that it sickens me. If I can't think about it now, how am I supposed to deal with it later?" My arms fold over my chest, and I grind my jaw. I tip back my head and stare at the ceiling, cocking my head to the side. My expression shifts as my eyes discover something I hadn't yet noticed.

Marty follows my gaze. "Wow."

"Tell me about it." My upper lip curls into a WTF expression.

"This is why no one ever looks up."

Marty and I stare at a nude painting of one of the lucky ladies that got into King Henry's pants. Who puts paintings on the ceiling?

We hear a laugh behind us and immediately turn. Mel and Henry are walking up the stairs, arguing about something, stopping when they see us staring.

Henry clasps his hands together and rushes toward us. "Isn't it lovely? It's a replica painting of Catherine Howard."

When I turn, I see Mel wearing a hoodie, yoga pants, and her trademark earrings. Her hair is slicked back and tied neatly at the nape of her neck. Next to her is Henry wearing a tweed suit that should belong in the 1920's. If he had a straw hat and a Dixie Band, he could be on Showboat.

"She's a child." I'm staring at the bony ass and girlish face above me. She appears to be between fourteen and sixteen years old. The angular features that appear on a woman's face after she's in her early twenties are missing.

Henry shriggles, half shrug, half giggle—his shoulders, not committing to either. He nods his head in agreement. "She is a bit young for my taste."

I gawk at him and jab my thumb up at her naked ass. "Then why is she on your ceiling?"

"Speculation?"

"Are you asking me or telling me?" I reply, wanting to slap him silly.

Mel groans. "Old, white man art. So he likes to stare at naked teenagers. Add that to his list of fucked up mojo."

Henry gasps and presses his hand to the ascot disappearing under his jacket. "How dare you? This painting is a masterpiece! Implying I'm a pedophile is uncalled for, you strumpet."

Mel snort-laughs, but keeps her mouth shut long enough for me to ask something I've been wondering about since last night. That drone. I'm hoping Henry is ahead of the game and has a tiny one around. I need it in case my plan goes to hell because they're not getting away this time.

"Yeah, that makes sense." I lift the corner of my upper lip and show a little tooth to Mel. She starts cracking up. I hurry on, not wanting to rile Henry too much, "It's reflective of the period."

"It is!"

"Exactly. Listen, I wanted to ask you something about the drones on your property."

He flinches and shakes his head, surprised. "I don't have drones." He says the word like they're disgusting.

Marty and Mel glance at each other and then back at Henry. Walking forward, stopping just in front of his wingtips, I smile and nod. "I mean flying robotic army. Like the ones you have patrolling your property."

"I know what a drone is, and I do not possess anything of that nature. Drones have to be registered with the FAA. I dislike that organization. Plus, I'm not a man who likes to flaunt his wealth." He smirks and tucks his hands into his jacket pockets, puffing like a paisley penguin.

"Why are you asking?" Marty steps up next to me and catches my eye.

A sinking feeling hits me hard before I answer. "There was one in the yard last night."

"What? Where!" Henry's voice is an octave too high. He's doing this jazz hands thing with his fingertips that I assume is annoyance.

"Back by the shed."

His head jerks back like I slapped him. "You were in the shed?" Henry folds his arms loosely over his chest and tips his head to the side. "Did you go upstairs?"

"Yes, you sick fuck. Why is there a bunch of Avery-sized stuff here? The clothing, creepy. But that could be a coincidence. The tank? Why the hell is there a tank, Henry!" Marty and Mel's eyes widen and both are mute—which is a first.

Henry laughs, tapping his fingertips together and stepping away. "You saw that, did you?"

"Yeah. I saw it." Marty senses the half-truth and gawks at me, jaw dropped for half a beat before he slams it shut. "What the hell is wrong with you?"

Henry looks bored when he stops fidgeting. "If you must know, I have a type. Short, wide hips, narrow waist, big hair."

"So you're saying that you could strap Mel into that thing?"

Mel jerks back like someone slapped her. "No one is strapping nothing on me. You're fucking crazy if you think I'll—"

Henry sighs and turns toward her. "As lovely as you are, you're not my type."

Mel and I yell in unison, "You just said—"

"Yes, yes, but she's not quite right for me."

"Excuse me," Mel snaps and gets in his face. "You wanna tell me why?"

His expression is cold and distant. "Very well, if you must know—although it's rude to point out—your hips are too full, your skin is too smooth, and your mouth too sharp. If you learned to be mute, I could forgive the other two."

"You sonova—" Mel winds her arm back, makes a fist, and nearly connects with the side of Henry's face. She jumps in the air to do it. It was very catlike.

Unfortunately, Marty decides to step in front of the douchebag and Mel clobbers the wrong guy. Marty isn't in the mood. He blocks the hit and tosses Mel on the carpet. She lands with a loud thump.

Marty sighs, doing this thing with his mouth where his lower lip is jutting up like it might eat his head. He's pissed. "Stay there!" he yells at Mel before turning on Henry and me. "You said you had no drones, but you said you saw one. Who's telling the truth?"

"I am." We reply in unison and then blink at each other, not understanding.

Marty closes his eyes and pinches the bridge of his nose. "Shit."

Chapter 13

"Who the fuck would fly a drone through your yard." Marty's question lacks the expected questioning tone, where he would normally elevate the pitch of the last syllable in the sentence. Instead, it's a demand laced with the threat of beating Henry senseless.

Mel grumbles, picking herself up off the floor. "The only reason I'm not kicking your ass is because I thought you were dead. I'm giving you a do-over. You're a thorn in my side, Mart-AN." She glares at him, nostrils flaring like she wants to rip him a new one.

I wonder if the two of them have more in common than they thought. How unnerving is it to have a dorky ninja sitting next to you day in and day out, never even once suspecting that he's lethal? Mel takes pride in reading people, in seeing through all facades. She's usually pretty good at it, but Marty makes her nervous. There was a time when she couldn't stand him and made fun of him relentlessly. That confident jibbing stops, replaced with grudging respect. It's freaking weird.

Marty rounds on her, his voice so soft and still it makes the hairs on my arms stand on end. "The thorn won't be quite so bothersome when you're dead, Melanie."

She sneers and cocks her head to the side while cracking her knuckles. "Fine, you wanna piece of me, white boy! Let's go!"

"Pardon me—" Henry starts talking at the same time as me.

"You two need to stop—" What the hell is he being polite for? Can I kill you with my manners? I'm starting to think the British thing is an act.

"—but if you get blood on the carpet—" Henry places a slender finger in the air.

"—acting like children—"

"—it'll never come out—"

"—and work together—"

"—believe me—"

"—right now!" I'm seething, as I stand between the two of them, which is probably a dumb spot to be since they both have weapons.

"I know." Henry wears a placid expression on his face. We all stop yelling and stare at him. He stands there aloof to anything odd and shrugs. "As if I'm the only person here who's killed a man? Just because I stand with criminals and lie among them, doesn't mean I want a fifty thousand pound carpet stained or worse."

Mel's jaw is hanging open. "What the hell is worse than blood?"

"Knives, you circus freak of a woman. You probably have them hidden on your person. A cut carpet is a nightmare to repair, so keep your street fighting where it belongs, outside with the other monkeys."

Mel's spine straightens like someone inserted a rod. Her mouth snaps shut as her eyes do this super-wide blink in slow motion before narrowing into thin slits. "What did you call me?"

Henry opens his mouth, "Why is she offended? She knows she's black, right?"

Marty laughs and steps back. His hands are in a surrender stance. "You're a dead man. Even if I stop her now, she'll just come back and finish you later."

Mel launches at him, springing through the air like a tiger. Henry makes a shrill scream, but it's all show. The man can fight, which wasn't evident before. He falls to the floor, and she straddles him, underestimating him. She doesn't see it yet. He didn't have to go down. He fell on purpose. This is going to end badly.

"Mel, stop! We need him!" I yell at her, but I don't want to get too close. "He's playing you, you idiot! Stop it!"

A flash of light reflects from a short silver knife in Mel's hand before she winds up to sink it in his side. When her arm swings out, Henry moves. He knocks Mel off balance, and her blade goes flying. Henry's actions are swift and well executed. She never saw it coming. He flips over her, pressing her to the floor, and crushing the air out of her lungs, before reaching out and grabbing her knife. He yanks her head by her ponytail, lifting her chin off the floor, exposing her neck. He pins her to the floor, face down, and holds her knife to her throat. If she swallows, she'll bleed.

Marty stands there, arms folded, letting them kill each other.

I throw my foot at Henry's temple while screaming at him to stop. He doesn't listen, and my kick does nothing to him, but it nearly kills me. It feels like I broke my foot. I need a fucking ninja!

"Stop this, now." Sean's voice is deep, steady, and even.

We hear a gun cock and everyone but Mel turns. He's standing there in tux pants and nothing else.

His arms are extended forward clasping the gun, aiming directly at Henry's head.

Chapter 14

Henry rolls his eyes, but he doesn't drop the knife, which is biting into Mel's neck. She doesn't make a sound, but there's a crimson trail of blood running down her mocha skin. "No one will miss her."

"I will," Sean says, surprising everyone. "As much as I want to put a bullet in your head, today isn't our day."

Henry inhales deeply, still doesn't move. "You like to take my toys."

"Amanda wasn't a toy."

"She wasn't yours, she was mine, and you broke her. I saw her toward the end, you know. Lifeless eyes and that growing belly. By the time you killed her, she was already dead." Henry stands and drops the knife on the floor next to Mel's head.

Henry mutters something as he walks away, tugging on his jacket and checking his sleeves for blood. If I didn't know better, he did that with Mel on purpose, like he was testing her. Why he took it that far is beyond me. There's no way he didn't know that calling her that wouldn't evoke an instant rage response, especially from her. The one thing Mel desires above all else is to be valued. She wants someone to see her for who she is and not use her because they can. I'm not sure what Henry was trying to prove, but Sean wasn't originally part of it. Those last few words were meant to get inside his chest and work their way to his heart.

Sean tucks the gun in the back of his waistband, walks over to Marty and inspects the cut over his eye. "You left me for dead."

"Ditto."

The corner of Sean's lips twitch slightly as if he wants to smile or say something, but he doesn't. He just turns to me and scans my body. "Are you hurt?"

"No." Yes, my foot is screaming like a crazy bitch in the mall on Christmas Eve.

Sean knows. His gaze drops to my foot. He doesn't ask, he just sweeps me up. "You need ice."

I smack him, protesting. "Put me down."

"Make me." His voice is flat, irritated.

He carries me down the stairs to the kitchen while Marty catches him up. Mel shrinks away in silence, no doubt embarrassed. Getting your ass kicked by a man wearing tweed had to be a shock.

We cross an enormous room, under the chandelier, beneath the dark stained, hand-carved coffers, and through a door that looks like part of the wood paneling surround the lower level of the room. I wonder how close Sean and Henry were at one point. They knew each other well, that much is clear. Henry knew how and where to hit Sean the hardest. Amanda is his weakest spot. He still blames himself. No matter what he says out loud, his feelings on the matter haven't changed.

After passing through a doorway, we enter a gigantic dining room. The table is a mile long. A plane could mistake it for a runway. The drapes are drawn, and we can see out the front of the house to the traditional English gardens. I can tell by the way things are planted and arranged. My mother always wanted a little English style garden but never got around to it.

On the other side of the room, we pass through another doorway, walk along a dark hallway, and into an industrial kitchen. It's the size of my parent's house. There are multiple stoves with griddles and burners. One wall of the kitchen has oversized double ovens in case you need to cook a dozen turkeys at once. Every cabinet is custom and resembles something from an old movie—or a Tudor palace. Even the racks hanging above the metal island are indicative of Henry's fetish. There are dead birds hanging there, dangling under the lights next to herbs and other things.

"Is that a duck?" No one answers me. It's too fat to be a wild turkey unless he went hunting at Heckscher and grabbed it off someone's barbecue. That wouldn't surprise me.

Marty hasn't stopped talking as he followed Sean and me across the large house. Marty's voice sounds annoyed. "He's not a civilian."

"I know," Sean sets me down on the counter.

"When were you planning on telling me?" Marty's voice drops and I wonder if this is the real him or if he's mimicking Sean.

Sean doesn't perceive Marty as a threat. He turns his back to the other man, going to the freezer hidden in a cream-colored panel and grabbing me some ice. He comes back with it wrapped in a towel and pulls my leg up so I can rest my foot on the counter before placing the ice on top.

Sean smiles at me and shakes his head. "Why do you think you're a ninja? You know you can't break a cinderblock with your head. Just thinking you can isn't what makes it break."

"Har, har. They were going to kill each other. What was I supposed to do?"

"No, they weren't." Marty's voice is firm. His arms fold over his chest as he stares at me. "He wanted to know what he was dealing with, and she underestimated him."

"Well, she won't do that again. She'll just kill him next time, no warning shot." I glance at my foot. Those little bones don't like getting hit hard. Kicking Henry in the face was like kicking a board. I wonder if he has a steel jaw.

"Which is what he was testing for," Sean explains, leaning against the counter next to me. He folds his arms over his bare chest, giving me a good view of the toned muscles flowing down his back. I want to lick the spot right below his shoulder blade, the place that's so tender on me—I wonder what he'd do.

"There's some misplaced loyalty there, enough to make her hesitate." Marty asks, "You think they know each other?"

"As far as I can tell, no. Neither one of them talks freely about their pasts, but I didn't find any connections between them."

"Maybe if you dig back through his records you'll find her?"

"Already did that. She's not there."

I roll my eyes. "Seriously? You don't know why she hesitated?" They gawk at me like I have a dog growing out of my neck, and it might bark. They both watch me, waiting. "She likes him."

Sean's eyes cut to the side, and he drops his arms. Marty steps toward me as they simultaneously accost me with questions. "How could she—"

"She hates him!"

"She beat the shit out him once already!" Marty adds.

I interrupt. "Right, and as you said, he's been playing it close to his chest, and she didn't know he could fight. No one catches Mel off guard, but plunging that dagger into his side bothered her, and we all know that nothing bothers Mel. Which means..." I place a hand in the air and unroll all my fingers at once for showmanship. "She's got a crush on the nutbag."

"That complicates things." Sean touches his jaw and walks over to the dead animal hanging over the island. "It's real. I know you were wondering. It's waterfowl. He probably shot it himself."

"The drones, I heard you say you saw one last night. Where?" Marty watches me, not realizing the type of information he's asking.

My face gives that away. Before I can respond, I feel it flame up, ear to ear. Super suck. I glance down and hear Sean laugh under his breath. "Back by Henry's freaky shed with no brooms."

"Sheds don't have to contain brooms," Marty interrupts. "Where's that rule written?"

"Don't even try," Sean says.

Marty nods, warned off, and redirects. "What did it do?"

"Nothing major," I say, thinking back. "It blinked, hovered, came back once more before zipping off."

"What were you doing?" Marty asks, prompting the memory of me being naked and kneeling in the doorway.

My face drops. It has a camera on it. Damn it. "It was taking pictures. Of me. In Henry's sick shed, and it never saw you." I glance at Sean before addressing Marty. "You thought something when I first mentioned it. What were you thinking?"

Sean produces a new cell phone from his pocket and starts web surfing. Marty glances at him and walks over to us. He's standing opposite Sean, who is next to me, hip leaning against the island. Marty mirrors the stance and folds his arms over his chest.

My stomach lurches up before falling into my shoes. I know what Sean's looking for, what he's going to find. "It wasn't Vic Jr's, was it?"

"No." His tone is clipped. He hands me the phone, and Marty leans in to see what pissed him off.

The page is a news rag that publishes celebrity gossip, and right there on the home page is a picture of me, blindfolded, kneeling on the floor stark naked worry etched on my face. I sneer and scroll down, finding several more pictures of me, but there's no sign of my name.

The article says that British Billionaire Henry Thomas imprisons women in a small house at the back of his property. It goes on to say they freed me, keeping my identity private to protect my rights. Wonderful. At least my face isn't showing. Everything else sure is.

"So, that's where you were," Marty looks smug when he straightens, "Being a toy for a fucked-up billionaire." He glares at Sean. "If you hurt her—"

I want to curl into a ball and die, but I don't. I kick my legs off the side of the counter and glare at each of them. "I chose Sean. Get over it." I smile when I say the next part. "But thanks."

Sean's triumphant smirk falls with that last word. "If you hurt me, Marty will kill you."

"Of course, Miss Smith. No brooms."

I make a face. "No brooms, ever. Splinters!"

Marty's eyes go wide, and he shakes his head, walking out of the room without a word.

Sean helps me down, and I wrap my arms around his neck and press a kiss to his lips. "So what's next?"

"We do a test run."

"Where? Isn't this illegal?"

He nods. "Yes, so we picked carefully and chose a common enemy. Information is power."

"So this is going to be a dry run, as in it's a similar setup to what I'll face at my brother's place?"

He pushes a lock of hair away from my face, nodding. "Yes, the system will work the same way, except we'll know Henry hasn't tampered with it because we're not knocking his home security grid offline."

"We're not?"

"No."

"Then whose house are we testing it on?" I can't imagine someone that wouldn't kill us or turn us in if things go to hell, and it doesn't work. Plus, they need to have a kick-ass security system. "It needs to be someone concerned about break-ins, someone with much to lose."

Looking at me from under dark lashes, Sean folds his arms over his bare chest and smiles darkly. "Exactly, which is why we're testing it out on the residence of pain-in-the-ass madam, Miss Black. She's got Manhattan by the balls. Whatever she's hiding at home is ten times more valuable than anything in her office. Plus, she hates me. With any luck, you and Mel can disable the system while Marty and I steal what we need to end her once and for all."

READY FOR MORE?
THE ARRANGEMENT 22
IS COMING SOON!

Make sure you don't miss it! Text HMWARD (one word) to 24587 to receive a text reminder on release day.

COMING SOON:

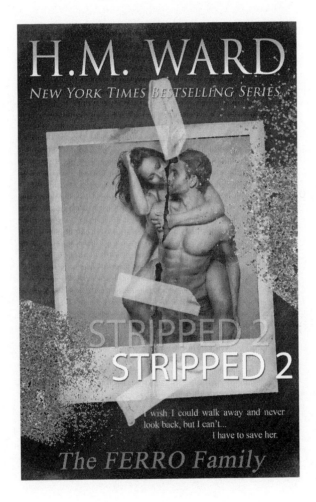

Pre-Order Stripped 2 Today!

MORE FERRO FAMILY BOOKS

TRYSTAN SCOTT
~BROKEN PROMISES~
******

JONATHAN FERRO
~STRIPPED~
******

NICK FERRO
~THE WEDDING CONTRACT~
*****

BRYAN FERRO
~THE PROPOSITION~
*****

SEAN FERRO
~THE ARRANGEMENT~
******

PETER FERRO GRANZ
~DAMAGED~
******

MORE ROMANCE BY H.M. WARD

SCANDALOUS

SCANDALOUS 2

SECRETS

THE SECRET LIFE OF TRYSTAN SCOTT

DEMON KISSED

CHRISTMAS KISSES

SECOND CHANCES

And more.

To see a full book list, please visit:
www.HMWard.com/#!/BOOKS

CAN'T WAIT FOR *H.M. WARD'S* *NEXT STEAMY BOOK?*

⭐ ⭐ ⭐ ⭐ ⭐

Let her know by leaving stars and telling her
what you liked about
THE ARRANGEMENT 21
in a review!

ABOUT THE AUTHOR
H.M. WARD

New York Times bestselling author HM Ward continues to reign as the queen of independent publishing. She has sold over 12 MILLION copies, placing her among the literary titans. Articles pertaining to Ward's success have appeared in The New York Times, USA Today, and Forbes to name a few. This native New Yorker resides in Texas with her family, where she enjoys working on her next book.

You can interact with this bestselling author at:
Twitter: @HMWard
Facebook: AuthorHMWard
Webpage: www.hmward.com

49253111R00076

Made in the USA
San Bernardino, CA
18 May 2017